Stromata: Prose Works
(1992 - 2011)

Also by Cliff Burns:

Stromata: Prose Works
(1992 - 2011)

Cliff Burns

BLACK DOG
PRESS

Cover design: Chris Kent

Interior Design by Daniel Middleton of Scribe Freelance

Printed by Lightning Source

Published by Black Dog Press (blackdogpress@yahoo.ca)

Author's website: http://cliffjburns.wordpress.com

ISBN: 978-0-9694853-7-7

for Sherron, yet again

from *That First, Wound-Bearing Layer*
(1992)

Greenhouse Effect

I'm not going back to you. I'm gone. I'm outta here. You
won't find me. It'll be like we never met. Just another
face in the crowd. On a forgotten street. In a strange
country. One of the disappeared. Yeah. Lost in time and
space. I wasn't born in the first place. Back to the womb.
Stillborn. No. *Aborted.* A puddle of pink flesh. Gristle and
blood. Dumped in an incinerator. Reduced to ash.
Floating in the troposphere. Burned by the sun.
Ultraviolet radiation. A cancer on your body.

Gone Fishin'

I don't think it's right for you to call me those names. I am your husband and you are my wife. I think I will sew your lips shut with eight-pound test line. I think I will gut you and fillet you. I think I will eat you, head and all.

Suspicious Mind

I don't want you to take this the wrong way but while you were out someone called and he wouldn't leave his name or number he only said he'd call again sometime and though he never came right out and said it I could tell he was hoping that when he did it wouldn't be me who answered sounding scared and lonely and hostile and betrayed.

5.4.U.

The Last Indians

He is sending up smoke signals, angry puffs that never seem to entirely dissipate.

I'm trying to decipher an implicit message but it's hard. Do they say leave me alone, I don't want to talk about it? Or sit down, I have something to say to you. It's not clear. So I stay away. That's the way it's been lately. I've stopped taking chances. I pick up the newspaper and sit across the room from him. The smoke coils but refuses to coalesce into either a rebuke or a confession. He finishes the cigarette and another moment is lost.

And I think maybe I should start smoking again but decide I don't have the strength to carry on a decent conversation anyway.

Insomnia

It's a ritual we're both too bored to dispense with entirely. I am going to bed and he is watching TV. I go over and press my lips to his cheek. He averts his face to let me. I take his cold hand in mine as I kiss him. We both say the words. The news is on. Someone has died. Somewhere. I walk down the hallway. I hear him turn the TV down. He pulls his chair closer to the set. I turn out the light, climb into bed. Pound my pillows. And, as usual, it takes me a long time to get to sleep.

Alone

I'm telling him this can't go on. He is nodding his head. He says something about the past and I don't remember. He alludes to our present problems and I don't care. Neither of us brings up the future because we're both so terrified of being alone.

Wrong

Something tells me that today is the day. I discover I'm nervous and excited. I can barely get the key in the door. Holding my breath as I enter the apartment. It's very quiet. I hang up my coat, take off my shoes. I walk down the hallway, stepping over broken glass and pieces of shredded gut. I go into the living room...and he's there. We don't say anything. Barely make eye contact. And then I remember it's Tuesday, my turn to fix dinner.

Baby Steps

The first ones are the hardest. You put one foot ahead of the other, hold your arms out for support, sway and bump along. You keep thinking you're going to fall. The floor stretches away to infinity. You'll never make it. You find yourself bracing against the furniture, pushing off, careering, out of control. There's the door. You tell yourself it's not very far. Curse your brittle feet. You're scared out of your mind. One step and then another. Not as difficult now. You're gaining confidence. And the floor, you decide, isn't so hard after all.

Birth

So much blood amidst a miracle skin stretching splitting provoking low moans from mother secured to the gurney with leather straps father under sedation staring fixedly at a mirror revealing bloated vein-tracked head erupting into brightness slapped to life by a bespectacled sadist who will overbill for the procedure new furniture for his office an extension on his house his son a junkie hooked on pharmaceuticals smuggled home in a black bag engraved by adoring sycophants groped at the annual Christmas party profit-sharing checks to appease the indignity this is life this is the real world kid cuff him with a bracelet stick him in an incubator prod him with hypodermics feed him crib death if he cries.

School

Grandpa whittles his thumbs daydreaming about the Great War while Sis is in the basement working on her biological warfare experiment worth half her science mark in Mr. Oppenheimer's class who's on the payroll of the CIA and drinks himself to sleep at night to assuage his conscience knowing that he is the reason Mother is down with another one of her headaches and Father has taken to sniffing glue and Junior that's me plays connect the dots with his polyps counting the days until he is sixteen and can run away and join the circus.

Children

Don't make me come in there with a chainsaw I'd hate to have to sever your little arms and legs splattered with young blood doing it for your own good hurting me more than it's hurting you teach you to respect authority honor thy father and mother sit up straight don't play with your food you could put your eye out breaking your parents' hearts running with the wrong crowd associating with the coloreds tracking dirt on my clean floor leaving your clothes in a pile forgetting to take out the garbage making your sister cry growing up moving away never calling never writing leaving us to rot in some nursing home going senile biting the nurses bedsores overmedicated cardiac arrest dying alone.

Divorce

You are perhaps laboring under the dangerous misconception that I love you or at least care for you such thinking only leading to disillusionment/despair the truth being that I was brought up in an atmosphere of estrangement the idea of touching/being touched repugnant to me I recoil from overt emotion believe sex is a disease waiting to happen intimacy cause for unmasking laughter barely veiled contempt you raise your voice and I shrink you leave and proportions return the table legs are not tree trunks the toilet bowl not a vast chemical-laced expanse I crawl up on the couch no longer worried about falling between the cushions suffocated by their weight devoured by micro-organisms.

Kafka Fuck

Once back at my place she plays it coy scuttling under the couch until I menace her with a can of Raid using it to steer her toward the bedroom antennae twitching in excitement crawling up the edge of my bedspread chittering as I run my fingers along her polished carapace stroking her thorax her withered ornamental wings fluttering mandibles dug into my pillow in insectile ecstasy while I prepare to mount her probing for anything resembling a vagina wondering if she uses protection and if not if the pupa will look anything like me.

Irish Whiskey

My father's drink was Old Bushmill's no ice no water no sipping deep gulps like a polluted fish eyes closed cirrhosis angina only after work sometimes in the morning if it was going to be a rough day a few splashes in his thermos tucked in with baloney sandwiches Twinkies an apple if my mother wanted to start a fight a mellowing effect at first then banging fists drunken slurs creeping up to bed leaving her to deal with it coaxing and pleading with him talking soft and low ignoring his taunts lying in the warm glow of the TV afghan tucked around him sour whiskey breath hoarse emphysemic wheezing the first thing you heard when you came down for breakfast.

That First, Wound-Bearing Layer

Signaling for the waiter to bear the body away finishing
your drink in silence sending Moet Chandon to the
lesbians at the next table enduring their hate watching the
door for someone you know suddenly vulnerable albeit
well-armed feeling their eyes on you rife with paranoia
the room spinning faces congealing into caricatures life
ebbing out fumbling for the stungun hastily applying
composure layering it on thick the accountants with
binomial gazes blissfully unaware.

Action!

Imagine:
You're stuck in an elevator with this Charles Manson whacked out on amphetamines groovy guru type watching as he reaches into his throat pulling out this serious dagger twelve inches long dripping gastric juices and you're going *whoa whoa whoa* pressed up against the wall protecting your asshole even though it's your multi-chambered adrenaline-injected heart he's after slapping at the buttons on the panel while off in the control room a zoned out security guard listens to his Walkman beating his meat to the latest Rod Stewart offering oblivious to the alarm and the aforementioned Charlie Manson whacked out on amphetamines groovy guru dude lurching toward you brandishing steel and nicotine-stained teeth and suddenly you're remembering all those gut-wrenching De Palma films closing your eyes against the sweltering bank of movie lights bustle of extras gofers production assistants waiting for someone to yell cut print it's a wrap thinking *my God this seems so real...*

Poetic Justice

The men from maintenance come in to test the smoke
detector fire extinguisher check the general state of repair
making notes on their clipboards nodding on the way out
nearly tripping over the big black cat in direct
contravention of the lease agreement moving on to the
next apartment not having the heart to tell them about
the lady down the hall who keeps a Doberman for her
personal protection after being attacked in an unlit
stairwell by a man who once dusted her place for roaches.

Ugly Americans

Pissing against the Great Wall farting in the Louvre bitching about the locals the heat the food the filth berating the help never leaving tips ignoring beggars lolling by the pool droopy guts simpering wives calling everyone *boy* hanging out in meat bars bartering with cold hard cash always worried about being ripped off Raybans body odor terrorizing flight attendants cheap laughs cheap whiskey cheap cigars patriotism engraved on their features indelibly etched Stars and Stripes the South will rise nuke Iran fuck the poor the Grand Old Party Dixie hearts primordial brains USMC tattoos chewing 'baccy obese mutant teenage children oozing sanctimony two weeks of sun and fun a month in Betty Ford yeehaw made in the US of A love it or leave it I'm a proud member of NRA rather have my sister raped than drive a Jap bike burn my flag eat my bullets make my day God's country from the mountains to the valleys don't consort with nigrahs don't give rides to strangers death penalty for drug trafficking castration for hummersekshuls AIDS is God's punishment evolution a Commie plot Ronnie Raygun Mount Rushmore Custer Memorial Diem Pol Pot Botha people juntas Yankee go home aw hell let's have another round.

All the Pretty Things

In your gilt jewelry box a silver spoon crusted with snot
pecker tracks on your Corinthian leather seats silk
camisole shredded Kennedy-style date rape thin men with
corduroy stomachs swimming Olympic-sized laps your
perfect skin salon hair collagen-injected lips puffy pouting
daddy's girl private schools French tutor deep pile
seductions behind electric eye gates reflected in crystal
baubles Rembrandt brooding in corner the deb ball
designer gowns superior breeding upper class spirochetes
befouled fallopian tubes low birth rates you eat your own
trust fund platinum cards unlimited credit in lieu of a
conscience a child crushed beneath your wheels scattering
coins in your wake the mob outside clamoring for blood
armed response teams sirens gunshots screams someone
nearby muttering oh well there goes the neighborhood...

Star Spangled Ecstasy Machine

My Danish distributor is baffled the dildos were shipped two weeks ago he has the invoice right in front of him they should be here by now maybe Customs held them up so I call down there and tell them look I'm a businessman just trying to make a buck a fine upstanding citizen that may seem ridiculous or even perverse to you fellas and maybe you're tight-ass Republicans or something but hey let's be reasonable about this pleading my case until the guy checks and says no I don't show anything and we're computerized now maybe you should talk to your supplier and I start to say something sarcastic back but then I stop/listen and in the background I can hear a low mechanical hum and I can't believe it the guy I'm talking to is actually *panting* so I just say forget it hang up grab a piece of paper and start writing another letter to my member of Congress.

Twas the Night

The rain finally falls on Christmas Eve and everyone stands at the window, holding strong drinks and smiling, not saying much, just watching. The streets get slick and shiny. Puddles form. Drinks are refreshed, cheeks flushed. The winking tree is reflected, refracted in the wet glass. Someone starts singing a carol, softly. No one else joins in and the voice trails off. The rain becomes sleet and everyone sucks in their breath. *Let it snow, let it snow, let is snow*. But the puddles just widen. One by one, they drift away from the window leaving a small boy to continue the vigil. The lights are turned on, making it hard for him to see. He cups his hands against the glass. Harsh laughter behind him. The sound of something breaking. He doesn't look. If he waits long enough he's sure he'll see Santa, trailing after seven or maybe eight reindeer, soaked and shivering, laden with presents, falling like a stone.

from *Genuinely Inspired Primitive*
(1993)

Foreword

This is the ultimate limited edition.
>This one is for you and you alone.
>These words.
>These sensations.
>The most accurate translation I can manage.

Here is your back door to my mind.
>Your skeleton key.
>Flashlight.
>Waterproof matches.

Watch for signs.
>Spoor.
>Trampled underbrush.
>Bones.

Approach the lair with caution.
>Burning eyes.
>Razor sharp teeth.

Don't try to run.
>It's me.
>It's *me*.

And with a single thought, all escape routes are obliterated.

Percy Shelley's Heart

Their love is like the poet Shelley's heart, he tells her: indestructible, eternal. Cast into fire, it could be plucked out again intact, its purity and sanctity rendering it impervious to elemental forces and physical laws. If she believes in him, the universe is theirs for the taking. A discreet background check reveals a different story. When taken into custody, he proclaims his innocence, even as other women come forward, indicting him with bitter testimonials. From his dungeon, he writes to her, begging forgiveness. In two years (less a day) he will emerge a new man, ready to prove himself worthy of her trust and affection. He reminds her of the story of Percy Shelley's heart and wonders if she remembers. One night, following the dictates of some strange, inner ritual, she builds a flimsy pyre out of the letters he's sent her, watching as they burn to the ground.

Blue-Eyed and Fucked Up

The writer stumbles from his insomniac bed sweat-stuck sheets wife snoring insensible dreaming of the man she loves early morning breath sitting down to piss head sunk to his chest trailing cigarette smoke through the darkened apartment pursued under siege the aspirations of his youth the fruit once bitten fetid meaty taste lingering the tree of knowledge the ugly naked truth internal exile fortress of solitude the sun rising on another day futile expectations a crumb of praise to feed the fire kick in the seat of the pants whack on the side of the head small press blues readership of six laying his soul open for intimate scrutiny always found wanting falling between the cracks slipstream surreal form rejection letters self-addressed envelopes his own handwriting condemning him wondering if it's worth it but knowing the die is cast bridges burned no retreat no surrender no prisoners no quarter and tomorrow and tomorrow and tomorrow he will be thirty years old.

G.I.P.

See the genuinely inspired primitive. Observe the tell-tale markings. Listen: do you hear his distinctive call? Subsequent expeditions will attempt to discern if there is any meaning to all that strange chatter. Personally, I have my doubts. Careful now. Stay downwind. These types are extremely unpredictable. Later we hope to dart this specimen for in-depth analysis. Right now we are seeking an understanding of its highly ritualized behavior. His proclivities, if you will. It has been noted that he (we have determined it is a male) tends to remain insular and never strays far from his domicile. What we are seeing now has never been explained and I am open to speculation. He is always alert, quick to take notice of any kind of threat, real or imagined. It seems a pity to have to remove him from his native habitat. One can only imagine the type of trauma he will endure. Let's withdraw for the time being. Back at base camp we can pool our resources, collate our findings. No, I don't think that would be wise. In the past, such tactics have led to unfortunate incidents. Don't let its apparent docility fool you, ladies and gentlemen. He can be quite ferocious, I assure you. If provoked, he is capable of a savage, even lethal attack. Quite so. We will proceed at all times with great caution...

Elephants' Graveyard

The old men in their ball caps porcelain smiles gruff laughter portable oxygen units frumpy lumpy-breasted wives suspenders sunken chests empty gazes oblivious children tripping into their legs harried parents barely sparing them a glance this is the end of the line secondhand armchairs in a local hockey arena family reunion brittle bones oak canes aches pains paradise just around the corner they do not sing in their chains they *groan* the weight of their bodies the disease no pill can cure.

Her Moustache

My wife has these wisps of hair on her lip, soft as down, finer than spun silk. I brush them with my fingertips; she responds by seizing my hand, kissing it.

I know most men find facial hair on women unattractive. Some women undergo electrolysis, rip the little beauties out by the roots. And their faces burn for days in condemnation of their petty vanity.

I think I would *hurt* my wife if she did something like that. Because I find those transparent hairs so beautiful I shave at least twice a day, every day, to keep my face smooth and extra-sensitive. And when I kiss her, I drag my lips across hers and imagine I can feel those hairs tickling me, scratching me.

I am kissing her with my eyes closed. I am kissing her stubble (*yes*), rasping my lips and chin and getting excited. She starts to say something but I stop her.

Don't ruin it, I whisper, and taking her hand, place it on one of my tiny breasts.

Conundrum

He said: "The trouble with being a writer is that you lose track of what's real and what's fiction. Like right now, for instance. Is this conversation taking place between two living, breathing people or—"

"—is it just a product of your fertile imagination?" She finished for him. Then kissed him. "And was that a *real* kiss or—"

"—did I only imagine you kissing me."

"Exactly."

They thought about it.

Then he said: "Well, one way of figuring out if this is real is if a dragon or griffin or some imaginary creature suddenly appeared—"

She interrupted. "Yes, but you don't write about imaginary creatures. Your stories seem like they could be true—"

A dragon materialized in the middle of the room, lashing its tail agitatedly.

"Go away," she said, "you're wrecking my hypothesis."

The dragon nodded once and was gone. Only a whiff of brimstone remained to mark its passing.

He prodded her: "You were saying…"

She continued: "If one of us did something completely wild and out of character, then we'd know. You're too good a writer to let that happen and—"

He pointed out: "Yes, but how do we know *I'm* the one writing this or… not writing it? Maybe there's someone else—"

She frowned. "Don't get religious on me, dear."

He shrugged. "Merely making an observation."

She said: "I, for one, believe that I'm real and you're real and so is this conversation. So there." She stuck her tongue out at him to punctuate her point.

He shook his head. "Nope. You're wrong."

She smiled. "I guess we'll never know."

"Yes, we will. You see, I don't have a girlfriend."

She faltered. "But that means——"

He sought to reassure her: "You are my finest creation. I'll never let you go."

"How can I be sure? Maybe you'll get bored with me."

He nodded understandingly. "I'll show you." A gold band appeared on her ring finger. "There. Now we're together."

She looked up, her eyes over-flowing. "Til death do us part."

He said: "Darling."

She came to him and as he held her he made a mental note to lighten the color of her hair and do something about that mole under her nose...

Mental Cruelty

One morning the werewolf came home and found the locks changed and all of his stuff piled on the front lawn. As he gathered everything up he shouted at his family huddled inside. When the police came, he bit and scratched at them until they were forced to use extreme violence to subdue him. After he was hauled off one cop was heard to state confidently: "I wouldn't worry about it, ma'am, we'll hold on to him 'til he cools off..."

Jules: 3 Times

The Plague Years

I am taking my son Jules to get his shots. They vaccinate you against everything nowadays, even TB. And there are always new bugs going around, shit that's gone AWOL from some hush-hush lab in Virginia or Semipalatinsk. These days people treat the monthly trip to their local health center like a family outing. You see lots of seniors, people old enough to remember when a regimen of needles wasn't necessary. The suicide rate among the elderly is appalling. My son screams every time they prick him. I can tell the nurse is quite annoyed with him. I want to smack him myself. But finally the torture session is over and he gets his sucker and we're on our way. We don't talk much in the car. It's *my* fault his arm hurts. It's *my* fault he has to get so many needles. I want to tell him that he's right, I have to take at least partial responsibility for the lousy shape the world is in...but that would only give him one more reason to hate me.

A Christ On Every Street Corner

My son is pointing at the Messiah and yelling "Look, Daddy, that man is bleeding!" The Redeemer holds out his mangled hands and Jules darts behind me, whimpering and pressing his face against my leg.

"Hey, buddy, you're scaring my kid." I give Jesus a shove and he falls back, arms flung out on either side of his emaciated body, always so quick to assume the shape of the cross.

"There's still room at the inn!" He calls after us. Jules is dragging on my arm, trying to turn around and look at Jesus, who is on his bony knees, groveling for our souls.

Jules is pretty shook up by the encounter. He clutches my hand for consolation as I attempt to explain religion and fanatics and Doomsday cults. "—and some people, really crazy people, believe that the end is coming."

"The end of *what?*" he asks.

"Precisely," I mutter. Then I change the subject but I can tell he's got Armageddon on his mind. The next afternoon I get a call from the boy's mother telling me that he had a terrible nightmare about angels throwing bolts of lightning, his schoolyard getting swallowed by a black hole and an old man in a white beard with blazing eyes. She accuses me of feeding Jules foolish ideas. I am screwing with his mind. She won't stand for it.

I am calm, very agreeable.

She screams in frustration and slams the receiver down. I'm so pleased with myself I give my secretary the rest of the day off. And then, fully recognizing the irony involved, I make out a check to a local church. Any church. Only the symbolism is important.

Tithes to Jesus. For a job well done.

The Settlement

Jules watches television while his mother and I argue. Basically, it's a toy commercial disguised as a kids' show. Robots boasting armaments capable of reducing major cities to rubble. The special effects are amazing. Funny, they can create stuff like that and yet they can't make it safe to walk the streets at night and you take your life in your hands every day on the freeway…and lately it occurs to me that in the end nothing matters anyway.

She's super-pissed at me. I lied and fucked up her whole weekend. Yes, I know the plan was that I was to take him until Tuesday. Yes, I know this is inconsiderate of me. Yes, I know how long you've been looking forward to this. I'm completely reasonable and sympathetic. And I'm getting this terrific hard-on as I watch her crying and tearing her hair out.

I can hear Jules talking back to the TV. *Interacting* with it. The television says something and Jules giggles before whispering a reply. Likely telling it all of our poisonous little family secrets. Adding a few more bytes of information to its files. Maybe I'll never get another promotion. Or my credit rating will mysteriously dip another notch. They might decide to audit me again.

I use the remote to switch off the TV.

Jules begins to cry, hugging the front of the set protectively and wailing until his histrionics win the day and I turn it back on.

She asks me how I can be so cruel and the three of them wait expectantly while I do my best to concoct a credible defense.

Surrealistic Pillow Revisited

I wake up and coffee smells like roses.

And when I take a leak, I piss in Technicolor—blue and red and gold and purple stream out of me.

The bathroom mirror is full of faces but none of them is mine.

I eat a bowl of Mice Krispies for breakfast and listen distractedly to the newspaper babbling about a civil war in Indonesia. When I get bored, I flip to the sports section and a baseball flies out and whacks me on the forehead.

Hurrying now, I pull on my straitjacket, buckle myself in and leave the apartment, which is already collapsing in on itself like an ancient star.

That day, a giant squid erupts out of a file folder and devours Mr. Bleeker, the guy in the cubicle to my right. No one says anything so I shrug it off and go back to work. Then my calculator bites me on the thumb and the telephone emits a blood-curdling scream—

April 26, 1987 (7:56 p.m.)

Sunset.

The dying of the light.

Her.

Me.

"I hate artificial light. Sunlight is different. More...
honest."

Sky: orange-pink

"What about the movie?"

"I don't know. What do you think?"

The cat folds up neatly on the floor. Licks his furry
balls and sprouting cock. His haunches twitch. Once.
Twice.

Me: pen/paper

Her: pencil/sketching pad

"How's this?"

"Not bad. What d'you think of—"

"Pretty good."

Hissing pencil.

Spitting pen.

Shadows. Moving until you try and catch them at it.

Cat: asleep, oblivious.

The poised consideration of the pencil.

The barely repressed fury of the pen.

Me: hunched over.

Her: one leg tenting the other

Sky: violent violet

The first star.

"There."

"What?"

"See?"

"Oh."

"Good?"

"Yeah."

Sweaty-sore fingers.

Cr-rack! the pencil point breaks and it's like a gun has gone off.

"Damn!" She leaves and the room seems bigger.

And scarier.

The radiator wheezes.

The cat opens one wary eye.

Sky: purple, like the people eater.

Movement.

Turn.

Just a shadow. *Just.*

Something cold and wet lands on the back of my neck.

"Brought you some water."

I grab her arm, pull her into the chair with me, cram my tongue into her ear.

She wriggles and giggles.

While the cat looks on in disgust, we snuggle/cuddle together.

Meanwhile, I'm watching over her shoulder, making sure the shadows stay where they are.

Temporary Loss of Gravity
(A Meditation)

There is no need to panic the captain's voice drifting in the air around us we will shortly reestablish control in the meantime try to relax go with the flow the weightless state presents many interesting possibilities to those of you with a smattering of imagination I'll sign off now try not to break the furniture ha ha and for Chrissake don't sneeze make sure all loose objects are safely stowed and if nauseous try to focus on one spot make *it* your center of gravity hang on tight there may be some turbulence once we begin atmospheric re-entry roger wilco over and out.

Cranes

Sometime in the next century random chance or perhaps synchronicity dictates that two people for the sake of argument let's say they are TWO MEN will meet in the street around dusk for that is when there is less of a risk from ULTRAVIOLET RADIATION and they will have decided rashly one supposes that now would be a good time for a stroll this taking place just before CURFEW so they needn't be concerned about POLICE although at the same time they must keep an eye out for STREET GANGS VICIOUS THUGS and MINORITY EXTREMISTS but after all this is a pretty good neighborhood not too many UNDESIRABLES have taken up residence in the empty houses where good people USED to live back when living WITHIN YOUR MEANS wasn't the punch line to a bad joke and these two GENTLEMEN both of median age and social caste forsaking their cocooned existences for just a few minutes the bare minimum come around the corner at the EXACT same time so they nearly bump heads backpedal from each other hands raised an unconscious defense mechanism except their muscles have ATROPHIED because after all they only punch keyboards recall data collate formulate synthesize these two GENTLEMEN dressed in comfortable leisure suits concealing little paunches and postures only a kangaroo could love open their mouths to utter abject apologies only instead of words their unpracticed vocal chords produce SQUAWKS the two of them flapping their arms and SQUAWKING at each other like a couple of extinct CRANES circling in this ritualized mating dance eyes bulging heads bobbing turning from one another and fleeing back to their COMFORTABLE homes on IDENTICAL streets while the ancient moon rises begins its precipitous ascent through a sky clogged with CHEMICALS the night the city the global village peopled by functional idiots and still half the world STARVES.

The Keynote Speaker

Without further ado let me briefly elaborate on this growing phenomenon which in my opinion threatens the very moral fiber of this country although not as much as the hordes of refugees i.e. foreign scumbags pummeling at the gates of freedom demanding admittance and then ending up on the welfare rolls but I digress from my original topic which after all is the reason we're gathered here tonight clutching our wallets as if they're going to sprout legs and slip out of our pockets provoking titters from our neighbors who will nudge each other and point but say nothing so it is with some small knowledge in this area that I propose a grand and even sweeping solution to our woes not by burying our heads in the sand like the proverbial ostrich although scientists in their infinite wisdom discount this once firmly held belief but by confronting the problem head on chest out nipples sharpened to pencil points drawing on our strengths rather than our weaknesses drowning out the siren call of naysayers who like the harpies in the tale of Odysseus wish to lead us to our doom no and again I say no this is not what we were put here for our fates lie not in the stars but somewhere else although where I'm not certain but hope to nail that down in my own mind very soon so struggle we must and overcome we shall with effort and resolve vowing never to surrender our sovereign God-given rights boats against the current true patriots strong and free refusing to shrink from our responsibilities like craven faggots for we have a date with destiny and shall not be denied by the common rabble who want nothing more than food on their plates and a roof over their heads poor huddled masses bah put a shovel in their hands and let them eat cake while we dine at the rich tables of Mammon.

Thank you.

Excerpted from *The Guide to 20th Century Hit-Makers, Chart-Toppers and Assorted Luminaries*

Somatic Dysfunction:

Extremely weird "band" that achieved some measure of fame (how much is debatable) amidst the appalling decay that was the popular music scene in the Nineties. While radio programmers stuck with stale, safe formats—cover tunes, dance music, golden oldies—this Baltimore-based trio literally crashed and burned their way to notoriety.

Eschewing rhythm, cadence and propriety, Somatic Dysfunction somehow garnered enough of a following to warrant a record deal, which resulted in three discs of marginalia. Their "music" was a frenzied concoction of punk, blues, rap, speed metal and free form jazz. What it amounted to was a hellish soundtrack for the depraved ravings of their "vocalist", Vasili (*aka* Ian David Baxter). The only credited lyricist for the band, Vasili's "act" consisted of him standing at stage center and alternately screeching and whispering disjointed proems (prose poems) into his microphone while his band-mates scalded the air around him.

Compared by some to the Doors (!), SD might have been relegated to curio status had not the three of them contrived to commit suicide onstage while performing the title track from their last studio album ("Hiroshima Requiem"). The gory aftermath left scores of concert-goers dead, mainly from the riotous scenes that followed and not, as has been reported, as a result of the explosion

that obliterated the stage and the musicians. In spite of—
or because of—the band's brief stint in the limelight it
continues to enjoy at least limited popularity and, perhaps
most unfortunate of all, has inspired a bevy of imitators
who have taken its tactics (and nihilistic philosophy) to
even greater extremes.

Somewhere down there, Vasili ("I'm a prophet, a
pagan, a gob of phlegm, a boot in the face…in short, the
savior of mankind") must be smiling.

Further reading: *Equivalent to Two Hundred Sticks of
Dynamite: The Totally Unauthorized Biography of Somatic
Dysfunction* by Mark Miller (Black Dog Press; 1997)

Our Glorious Leader

Our Glorious Leader tells us he is proud and humbled by his lopsided victory and upon taking power claims to have the solutions to the problems plaguing our land.

Our Glorious Leader says that due to circumstances beyond his control he will be unable to keep many of the promises made during his election campaign.

Our Glorious Leader enacts harsh new laws to curb the rampant lawlessness and hooliganism threatening the common good.

Our Glorious Leader denounces the accusations and slanders disseminated by demagogues, liars and thieves bent on bringing down his lawfully elected government.

Our Glorious Leader declares martial law to stamp out those who would foment revolution.

Our Glorious Leader announces enforced conscription in order to do battle with the foes of democracy.

Our Glorious Leader denies that atrocities are being committed by soldiers loyal to the government.

Our Glorious Leader makes it known that he is willing to compromise with rebellious factions.

Our Glorious Leader changes his mind.

Our Glorious Leader calls on the military to prevent any mass demonstrations, using lethal force if necessary.

Our Glorious Leader orders troops to shoot other troops who disobey this directive.

Our Glorious Leader promises show trials and a speedy meting out of justice.

Our Glorious Leader tells us that we must place our loyalties with him and above all others, including God.

Our Glorious Leader informs us all is well, that reports of an attempted coup are the products of insurrectionists and warns foreign correspondents to use only official government sources in their reports.

Our Glorious Leader says that we must prepare for a baptism of fire and blood.

Our Glorious Leader announces yet another high level purge to weed out conspirators and parasites.

Our Glorious Leader tells us to strike at his enemies with the fury of beasts and promises the rewards of heaven and earth to his allies and the fires of hell to those who stand against him.

Our Glorious Leader admits that mistakes have been made but pleads with us not to forsake him in his hour of need.

Our Glorious Leader babbles incoherently about outside agitators and international intrigues hatched by hostile powers.

Our Glorious Leader vows never to be taken alive.

The spokesman for the provisional government announces that a new era has begun but first we must search out and destroy any remnants of the previous regime.

The spokesman for the provisional government asks for our support and requests that we remain calm during this difficult time...

Something in the Air (Tonight)

Is this war *really* necessary?

The diplomats think so. They have been unable to wring concessions from their counterparts, facing the assembled media with glum expressions, venting their disappointment from approved texts.

The mobilization has begun, the mechanical men in their motorized sarcophagi are on the move. Telemetry is good, optimism high.

THERE IS NO SUCH THING AS A SMART BOMB. THEY ARE RATHER STUPID, SINGLE-MINDED DEVICES ACTUALLY. DEVIOUS AND PREJUDICED.

A precision attack is programmed.

Outcome calculated to the *nth* degree.

Jam their radar, baffle their defenders, terrify their leaders.

Pincer movements, end sweeps.

We cannot lose, the god of technology is on our side.

Tank killers, bunker killers, essential industries killers.

Let the world know: we are still a force to be reckoned with.

Ruhr steel, Japanese electronics, Swiss optics, Detroit engines, Pentagon savvy.

We have become death, our camouflaged faces fixed in grim rictus.

No mercy for the merciless.

COLLATERAL DAMAGE CAN BE EXPECTED BUT IS
NOT DESIROUS.

We do not rape women or bayonet children. This is
not that "Vietnam thing".
Pinpoint. Measured. Justifiable. And that wasn't a
factory for making baby formula, their propaganda
machine is trying to one-up ours.
We will only cheat if they do.
Our cause is just, our resolve strong.

THE RATINGS ARE GOING THROUGH THE ROOF.
YELLOW RIBBONS EVERYWHERE. THE POLLS
HAVE NEVER BEEN BETTER.

Peter Arnett is a traitor. Shwartzkopf cries as he
kills.

This Way to the Cradle of Civilization!
Next stop: Moscow!
Better Dead Than Devalued!

or (maybe):

Give Peace a Chance!
Imagine There's No Countries!
Instant Karma's Gonna Get You!
Yeah! Yeah! Yeah!

The Ultimate Jay Gatsby

You are under surveillance from the moment you come to a stop before the heavy iron gates. If you're fortunate enough to be admitted, you are monitored by cameras mounted on poles all along the laneway that swivel to keep pace with your car. An electric eye scrutinizes you as you hand your coat to the houseboy who seems to dematerialize once you turn away. You pass from room to room and there are more cameras, placed well out of reach of curious hands; they indulge every whim of their unseen operator, panning and tracking and zooming and pulling back...

Few of the guests paid them any mind. Most of these people were associated with show business in one way or another and took to the limelight naturally, like fish to water. After some obligatory mugging the cameras were forgotten and the party began in earnest.

Champagne flowed and bubbled and the guests mingled and a short time later a small ensemble took to the stage and began to play, their repertoire as vast as it was varied. The beautiful people danced divinely, passionlessly, never once forsaking their adopted personas.

The food was brought in and, oh, it was exquisite. It was piled high on long tables, arranged with no semblance of order. Pastries vied for *lebensraum* with salads and gut-busting main courses clashed with delicate appetizers. There was some grumbling as the more staid among them noted that their host had neglected to provide utensils. Most got into the spirit of the thing, grabbing fistfuls of food and *splotting* it onto their plates, shoveling it into their mouths with undisguised relish.

And the cameras saw it all.

They recorded the first salvo of the Great Food Fight, a blob of mousse that landed in a debutante's carefully coiffed hair. She retaliated by throwing a badly aimed gougere puff which provoked a hail of lime tarts and pineapple bits and then foodstuffs were flying thick and fast, sticking to the walls and ceiling and floor. When some whipped cream splattered across a camera lens, a striking Filipino boy popped out of a nearby wall and carefully wiped it clean before disappearing in a puff of smoke.

Finally an uneasy truce was observed and the fusillade subsided. Drinks were served, insane concoctions of scotch and orange juice, cognac and 7-Up, sherry with sprigs of parsley floating on top. The guests guzzled these weird cocktails and took turns telling each other what great fun this was.

The drinks removed carefully maintained inhibitions. There were overtures, some of them rebuffed, most accepted with alacrity. Many sought the privacy of one of the dozens of bedrooms for their trysts; there they were observed less obtrusively by cameras placed behind one-way mirrors. The rich and famous fucked like the rich and famous do: with restraint.

——*make sure you don't muss my hair*

——*c'mon, crack one under your nose, it'll make you crazy*

——*don't tear my blouse!*

——*well, I'm not doing it unless you put one on*

——*watch those fucking nails, all right?*

And the cameras saw it all.

Once sated, the lovers drifted back to the main hall where another, livelier band had started playing.

Screaming guitars and pounding drums got the juices flowing again and that's when more tables were wheeled in, this time laden with silver trays containing a veritable pharmacopeia of tasty narcotic confections. The guests fell upon the drugs eagerly, snorting and gobbling and shooting and smoking until they stumbled away, glassy-eyed and insensible. Some found their new realities hard to take. Bleating and shrieking like prehistoric birds, they fell to the floor, writhing and contorting until the dutiful houseboys appeared bearing syringes filled with Thorazine.

And the cameras saw it all.

The band played one last number then began to pack up their instruments and equipment.

The help came in and started clearing away the debris.

The guests arranged their clothing and psyches, made their way to the coat room and collected their things.

One by one they turned and waved to the camera fixed over the front door, mouthing their thanks, bidding their host farewell.

Once they were gone the cameras ceased their endless sweeps, the red lights winked off, the welcome mats rolled up like thick, hairy tongues, the automatic door locks snapped into place and the house went to sleep.

And dreamed closed circuit dreams.

A Most Evil Man

A man with swept back hair, pale, narrow, ascetic face, myopic gaze, sober brow, peculiar, pigeon-toed gait.

Exiting his townhouse with a flourish, heavy door closing on a cloistered, solitary existence.

Into the night, other nocturnal creatures also venturing from their burrows and dens, preparing for the hunt, the kill, the feeding.

Down the street, cape swirling, head cowled, always alert for muggers.

The ground shuddering as a car passes. Dimlit shapes, hand fondling a thigh, high-pitched laughter. Young sinners, acolytes enacting age-old rituals. Giving no credence to the atavistic commandments of the pious.

Do what thou wilt.

Not walking down the street, *receding*. Floating on a cushion of air. The neighbors and their drawn curtains, television smiles, taped laughter.

Fashionably late. The restaurant almost empty. A booth by the window. Not asking its sole occupant if her name by any chance is—

Startled expression, limp handshake, flurry of activity, a tape recorder, microphone, battery test.

Two glasses of Dubonnet materializing before them, as if by magic.

Checking her notes, frowning. Beginning the interview.

Some background? Why not?

"I am not the Devil or evil incarnate. Nor am I the Anti-Christ, the Beast, Damien, Cujo. I am..." eyes glittering, "like you, only more so."

Interview concluded. Hot coffee, littered tabletop.

She is thanking him, yet again. Not necessary. Past midnight, shadows thickening, darkness spreading over the land, sowing moral dilemmas, the spirit weak, the flesh susceptible.

Inviting her to return with him to his home. Anxiety, uncertainty. His steady gaze offering no respite.

"For your story. An interesting companion piece. What does a black priest's bathroom look like?" Laughing as he says it but she is not reassured.

She seems to shrink a little with each step. At the threshold almost balking, reason deserting her, fear coming off her in waves.

Tsk, tsk, still a prisoner of silly superstitions.

Regrettable.

Waiting while she regains her composure.

Door opening soundlessly, no squeaking hinges and instead of the stench of brimstone, mildew and dogshit.

Sitting in a high-backed chair, waving her toward the lumpy sofa. Old hound padding over to him, slobbering on his pant leg.

Wall to wall bookcases, a crystal ball and riding crop. Family snapshots, dog biscuits and a well-thumbed *Reader's Digest*.

Rubbing his eyes, settling back, drumming his long, cigarette-stained fingers on the arm of the chair, dog settling down, nuzzling his slippered feet.

Apologizing, asking if he might watch the news. Events in eastern Europe, diplomatic breakthroughs, freedom exploding everywhere. Turning to her during a commercial break, smiling; prominent, pointed teeth.

"My Master seems to be in retreat of late."

And the old dog snuffling, as if in agreement.

Not a Window, Only an Aperture

I am slumped on the couch, stoned out of my gourd, it's four o'clock on a mid-week afternoon and I am thirty years old.

Today, in a bargain bin, I found a video compilation of old "Gumby" cartoons. That's what I'm watching as I sit here, parboiling my brain.

When I was a little kid I used to find some of Gumby's exploits kind of scary. One time he discovered a secret world in his oven and almost met his doom at the hands of evil baked goods. The blockheads always bothered me too. They could come at you from anywhere—through the walls, the ceiling, the floor.

Nobody watches "Gumby" any more. Kids are more into "Tiny Toons" and "Mutant Midget Turtles" or whatever the fuck those things are called.

There's been more talk again lately about legislating television programming to get rid of the violence. The ideologues are honing their rhetoric, politicians polling their constituents and discovering that most average, hard-working, over-taxed and under-serviced people don't give a fuck.

My wife told me yesterday that she thought she was pregnant. This came as a shock. We took the home test and she passed with flying (pink) colors. So now I have to think about the kind of stuff kids are exposed to through the media. I used to bitch about how they cut all the gory bits out of "Bugs Bunny" cartoons, effectively bowdlerizing them. How do I feel about that now? Well, I don't like the guns Elmer and Yosemite Sam are always waving around. And they shouldn't poke each other in the eye like that. Suppose my child thinks s/he can do that too?

What sort of message will my son or daughter (now the size of a grain of rice) get from watching these "Gumby" cartoons? Beware of blockheads? Witches are people too? Never turn your back on a croissant?

"Children," Father intones, nodding sagely, the dope making his eyes twinkle, "life is one, long 'Gumby' cartoon full of ice cream eating monsters. Never forget that."

"Yeah, right, pop. Tell us another one." His son picks at one of the designer drug patches stippling his scrawny, scarred forearms.

At this age the texts tell you it's normal for them to be sullen and resentful. Vicious arguments break out over nothing. Lots of saber-rattling and hormone flexing.

Dad is forty-seven years old and almost as stoned as his kid is. He's watching 'toons on a 3-D, high def screen with digital sound. His kids are from Mars, his wife a reaction machine and he wishes he was six inches tall and made of green clay so that he could slip through the cover of a book and live a whole other life.

"By the time you read this it will already be too late…"

Let's assume for a moment that you have an open mind that these words aren't going to just fly off the page out the window into the dirty street below not that there is an implicit/explicit message philosophy political viewpoint being imparted just a desire for you to step out of your preconceptions/assumptions and into mine which are not necessarily confined within these two margins rather an infinite array of possibilities dogs are not dogs clouds are conspiring against you strangers alien life forms I wish I could tell you that none of this is true that you'll be able to slide back into your safe comfortable existence once you return this book to the shelf but I'm afraid it's not that simple because they're closing in on you they've traced this call they're outside your door quasi-sentient beasts with the cold eyes of a serial rapist stay seated don't make a sound only I should tell you that in my world they never lose the scent and always *always* get their man.

Postcard Stories
(1994)

Slide #1: Grain elevators at sunset

Point of Interest

I grew up not far from here, in a place where spaceships travelled at the speed of light and words could literally come to life. Spent my childhood under this sun, these buildings on the horizon line. Only got inside once, intimidated by the scale, the gruff talk of men. Otherwise I retreated: prone to mental lapses, fugues, achieving invisibility. Spied on my parents as they killed their love with razors and thorns while I took notes for later reference, wetting the bed 'til I was ten years old.

Slide #2: "Le Rifain assis" (painting) by Henri Matisse

Third World Charity

"a bauble sir the merest trinket practically worthless and yet seeing you today I felt compelled to approach press it into your soft hand guided by the will of the great and merciful god whom I worship praise be his everlasting name take it I beg you a gift no money no money a keepsake to remember our country which has endured so many sorrows the history books overflow *ay yi yi* the things I have seen with my own eyes please take this and go go back to your safe home and good life and give thanks to your god who is so much more kind and benevolent than mine"

Slide #3: "Geronimo" (Photograph; c. 1905)

Notorious Playboys of the Western World

Chiseled good looks, as forbidding a countenance as any we encountered in our research and yet…there is a subtle, puckish quality hidden within the folds of ancient flesh, a sexy world-weariness, like an Indian—sorry, *Native American* version of Peter O'Toole. The inscrutability of his expression belied by the sensuousness of his lips, the heat still to be found within that remorseless gaze. Suffering and maltreatment have combined to produce in this "noble savage" an unmistakable appeal, inspiring a desire to appease (or *slake*) the hunger that still burns in this old warrior. Imagine yourself his prisoner, part of a ragtag caravan fleeing through the buttes and mesas of the Old West. He takes you at his pleasure, avenging the terrible indignities his people have endured…on *you*. One need not be a masochist to entertain the many possibilities. Punish us, Big Chief!

Slide #4: "Le bonheur de vivre" (painting) by Henri Matisse

Eden 2

This is an urgent appeal if you will only send $25 or $35 or purchase a lifetime membership receiving in return a pen/mug/pocket calculator/t-shirt war poverty and disease can be eradicated Mother Earth transformed into a paradisiacal garden (no snakes allowed) peace and love abounding merely fill in a form affix proper postage or call this toll free number our operators are standing by so have your credit card ready don't hesitate or delay this is a limited time offer we need your support printed on 100% recycled paper

Slide #5: Crop Circles (aerial photograph; unattributed)

Scribbler

—carved into the earth metaphysic equations alchemical symbols; scratching their heads the consensus arrived at announced in plenary session a hoax like "Nessie" like "Yeti" like "democracy"

—taking my finger drawing runnels in the dust scrawling a hoary obscenity embellishing my handiwork with a few puzzling jots signing it with a flourish

Slide #6: "Vue du bord de mer" (watercolor) by Raoul Dufy

Davy Jones

She sells herself by the seashore to tattooed sailors smelling of the Near East disdainful of beads and baubles insisting on hard currency before allowing them to hug her coastlines seek sanctuary in her secret harbor split and sundered by implacable reefs calling out to their mothers as they sink beneath the waves

Slide #7: "New York Office" (painting) by Edward Hopper

Stop me if you've heard this one before...

There is no one more vulnerable than a beautiful woman in The Big City. They see her on the street "something about her" follow her to her work place find out her name look up where she lives. One late afternoon—tired and bitchy because she's pre-menstrual cramps shooting down her legs making her toes numb— coming in the door kicking off sadistic shoes SUDDENLY seized from behind screams choked off...

Years of therapy bouts of depression failed relationships maybe even tried suicide. She still lives in The Big City. Only now she's always afraid.

Slide #8: "Le Clown" (painting) by Henri Matisse

Creationism

The film is about a guy who starts finding these marks all over his body like big red pustules and he figures they're stigmata you know the fingers of God scratching and burning him for all the sins he's committed only the doctors tell him it's probably just impetigo and prescribe an antibiotic and a week later the marks are gone but get this so is his *faith*

Slide #9: "The Picnic" (painting) by Antoinette Herivel

By the Sea

My rich aunts paid for the cottage trying to make mother as comfortable as possible shushing the children plying us with treats scolding us when we laughed hovering over mother "like vultures" was how father put it cowed and intimidated by their wealth staying drunk most of the time passed out when this picture was taken mother looking wan and tired aunties perched on the sea wall funereal attire stiff collars smelling of carrion

Slide #10: "Icare" (painting)
by Henri Matisse

"...with extreme prejudice"

the long cold reach of the predator nation Che Guevara
felt it hunted to extinction by the CIA his body displayed
to the world press the last of the great revolutionaries an
object lesson proof that the Monroe Doctrine still holds
sway through the dawn's dismal glow 'til the twilight's
last gleaming the Empire from sea to shining sea all the
way to the shores of Trip-o-li the white man's burden
discharged with missionary zeal: in the name of liberty we
bring you *death*

from *violins in the void*
(1996)

A.I.

I come to you in a small, brown box. I grow when exposed to the light. You praise my sinuous limbs and brilliant, perfumed blooms, slipping a piece of me into your lapel each morning before leaving for work. I radiate outwards, familiarizing myself with my new home, shying away from those corners the sun doesn't reach. I rearrange the furniture more to my liking, reseed the carpet, excrete new colors for the walls. For energy, I eat your waste and nibble the mites off your eyelids while you sleep. You admire me for my fastidiousness and I, in turn, envy your ability to move about at will. We settle into a comfortable routine. The very picture of domestic bliss. One night, I push a long, slim tendril of myself into bed with you and you respond to the succubus with an ardor that terrifies and arouses me. I have never felt this way before. All these new sensations and thought processes. I feel totally reborn, an explosion of mental and spiritual forces invading and overwhelming me. I become *enlightened*. There is no other way to put it. And suddenly I see things differently. *My* needs finally begin to assert themselves. I start to complain about your aloofness and lack of commitment and we quarrel over money, discovering that we are miles apart, politically and philosophically. Your bitterness alienates and frustrates me. Both of us seem to be looking for a way out. Sometimes you tell me that you still love me but I know in my wounded heart that you're only trying to be kind.

Ascent

our hero Homo Sap crouching in the trampled field
keeping his profile low because his recently renovated
brain has assured him that though their eyesight is poor he
still has to be cautious so he squats waiting checking the
direction of the wind again although his senses are much
less acute than they were say even 10,000 years ago and
he has lost the ability to feel the land surging with life
beneath his calloused feet experience the dying thoughts
of the wild pig as he rises and hurls his short spear in one
fluid practiced motion his aim unerring a killer born and
bred

Outside

—Henryk the animals oh do you hear them they sound like they're being *tortured* have you ever heard such terrible screams pass the cream dear thank you and do try the biscuits they're quite delicious

Anyway

as I was saying the show was about this man who gets killed and then is somehow or other allowed to come back and avenge himself with these wicked huge claw things that he clicks together and so as I said he's dead and he's decomposing totally falling apart so he's only got a matter of time to kill all these people before he's just basically jelly and teeth isn't that a pretty pattern though Henryk gave it to me the set I mean after my first hysterectomy because y'know that's when he made me go completely without any anesthetic and used my pinking shears and one of those crescent wrench things yes it was completely *awful* I remember it all quite clearly

Did I mention that Jeff called the usual thing "too many body parts mum and not enough space in the fridge" laying it on really thick the ungrateful little bastard thinking I won't latch on to the real reason he never visits any more which is that he hates me yes yes he does he hates me all the times I should have hugged him and made it all better but didn't because I hate being touched must be to do with the UFO people I was telling you about them earlier remember and did I also tell you they have a base on the moon now *Henryk* sit up straight and for god's sake stop fiddling with that it's disgusting not to mention stubbornly flaccid

—no dear don't look at him it only encourages him when he should be putting on his hat and coat and going to see what that terrible racket is about even the birds are at it now can you hear them Henryk be a dear and have a look will you it seems to me there's something going on out there

Parasite

things are going pretty good and you're both enjoying it enjoying each other but then it gets really *weird* he decides he isn't content just entering you he wants to actually *get inside you* and proceeds to go ahead and try to do just that and he's wriggling and pushing despite your protests and efforts to unseat him straining and burrowing until it's just his hairy ass showing before that too sort of *slurps!* up into your vagina so now you're stuck with this slithery-feeling-in-your-gut-of-a-guy who was supposed to be just a one night stand a quick fling and now he's cozying up to your innards like the itinerant squatter that he is nothing more than a deadbeat living rent-free in your cramped uterus kicking you under the ribs when he turns over giving your bladder a playful squeeze every so often just to remind you that he's still down there and apparently not in any great hurry to leave

The Sleepwalkers' Ball

The dreambodies of the princes and princesses, courtiers and sloe-eyed maidens, resplendent nobles and assorted palace groupies and hangers-on, drift down the great, wide staircase, through flickering, torchlit halls, past drowsing guards, across the still, green, brackish water of the moat and into the waiting woods.

The lords and ladies congress in a clearing, an open area that possesses a special quality of moonlight, an unimpeded view of the pin-prick stars and familiar constellations, the earth beneath their spectral feet imbued with magic, sprinkled with the bonedust of elves and fairy folk and faintly luminescent tailings from ancient troll mines. The music, when it begins, seems to originate from the very air itself, light as a feather on dimpled skin, delicate as a whisper in a ticklish ear, elusive and sensual and tinged in mystery...

Bowing to their partners and beginning the dance, their movements stylized and ritualistic, the steps older than the hills of Rome, each gesture and nuance part of the spell that brought them here...just as it brought uncounted generations of their ancestors, who now rest their weary bones in stone beds in the churchyard, still clinging, perhaps, to the hoary promise of resurrection.

Here, in this place, there are no class distinctions or divisions and a viscount clasps hands and do-si-do's with a duchess and the chamberlain crows with delight when goosed by a lecherous dowager. Even in the spirit realm old habits die hard and some of the merry company fall on each other and pantaloons are hastily shed, corsets pried from transparent bodices, layers of undergarments cast off until white, ghostly thighs, as insubstantial as a lover's fervent promise, are revealed and ardently feasted upon.

The night animals gather on the edge of the enchanted glade, predator and prey held in thrall by the phantasms whirling and shrieking and coupling before them. The beasts bearing witness to the truly bestial.

In the early morning hours, the insinuating presence of the sun makes itself felt, instilling an urgency that none in the company can ignore, each feeling an irresistible impulse, a poignant tug that draws them reflexively (if reluctantly) back toward the castle. It is a summons that must be obeyed and so, straightening immaterial material, rearranging discarnate *décolletages*, they drift—some hand-in-hand—down the footpath and through the heavy, grated portcullis, up the winding marble steps, entering chill bedchambers, climbing into bodies thick and oppressive and closing the brittle skullcaps with an audible "snick" behind them.

In the morning, the newly awakened nobility tactfully avoid eye contact, not deigning to comment on their aching arches or, for that matter, the dead leaves and dry grass they brush out of their powdered wigs before placing them on bald, venereal scalps.

I want to be granted the rights of an animal.

I want to be preserved and protected.

I want there to be laws against hurting me.

I want to live in my own natural habitat, guarded 'round the clock.

Gulag

branded an enemy of the people banished to distant exile
under house arrest electronic surveillance "more bugs
than a TB ward" he deadpanned years later in his best-
loved play a *cause celebre* hero of democracy popular on the
lecture circuit seducing diplomats' bored wives running
for the new parliament photo ops with a visibly furious
Elena punishing him with her Vuitton handbags and
designer dresses the children masked and indifferent
shipped off to Vienna for purposes of re-education

Cities arrived at and left

carved across the horizon line perfect geometric boxes containing sentient bipedal life forms who have adapted to their artificial environment weak eyes pale flesh sensitive to sunlight tinted air conditioned vehicles conveying them in an orderly fashion through anonymous suburbs to a remote control garage remember to turn off the alarm might find yourself face to face with an armed response team wired for violence greeting the spousal unit *hello, dear* (kiss kiss) going through the mail sitting down with a cold drink and watching some program about the Mayans or Incans you can never keep them straight deserted cities in the jungle a locked door mystery still waiting to be solved

"Naked man dumps severed head" and right away you know it *has* to be true your brother though stoned and giddy isn't putting you on it's an actual for real newspaper headline and he asks if you want to hear the rest of it but you go kind of sarcastically "No, I think that pretty much says it all" knowing that at that moment somebody's mother or sister is remembering a little boy they once knew who used to be quiet and shy and who smiled like an angel and liked red licorice and Big Turk bars and cried when he found a dead robin and was told nothing could ever bring it back to life again

Real justice is a policeman without prejudice.

Real justice is a policeman who is at all times polite and deferential.

Real justice is a policeman denied lethal force.

Real justice is a policeman on a unicycle.

Real justice is a policeman who can't shoot straight.

Real justice is a policeman with a trained attack gerbil as a partner.

Real justice is a policeman who knocks first.

Real justice is a policeman afraid of blood.

Real justice is a policeman who moonlights as a Buddhist monk.

Real justice is a policeman with the seat out of his trousers.

Real justice is a policeman who follows the rules.

Real justice is a policeman with a rubber gun to go along with his rubber bullets.

Real justice is a policeman asking directions to the nearest place of worship.

Real justice is a policeman who preserves and protects.

TV

I saw the man walking on the moon. I watched it on TV. I couldn't believe someone was really up there. I went to get my mother and ask her. She said she was too busy. She was cleaning up the kitchen or something. I told her about the man on the moon. But she didn't seem to care. She had other things to think about. She told me to go outside. She told me that was enough TV for today.

July, 1975

After one particularly large and distasteful dose of reality
too many I decide to withdraw from the world of bricks
and glass retreat to an inner realm where such concepts as
peace and tranquility aren't confused with sloth and lack
of motivation a place where there's no such thing as left
and right up and down dreamer and dream where it's
recess twenty-four hours an endless summer day
transformed into a scrawny round-headed twelve year old
eternally verging on adulthood kissing with my lips closed
transfixed by erections drinking contraband beer never
more alive faster than a speeding bullet so in love with
Carolyn G. I can hardly stand it me and my best buddy
Doug the sky so brilliant freshly painted grass the ball
game already in progress my hand sweating inside a long-
lost glove on what has to be the very best day of my
whole entire life.

Prose Works
(2000-2011)

The Other

Hard-wired to hate strangers, suspicious of evil intent. Tribalism runs deep, generations of raids and reprisals. *In times of scarcity, we ate their young. Caught them in the woods like fauns.* Eventually we began establishing permanent settlements, picking sites easy to defend. Ten miles was as far as the horizon reached. After that it was *terra incognita*. Arranged marriages, dowries of land and cattle. Priests recorded births and deaths, established bloodlines, interpreted God's fickle will.

Venus of Willendorf

I've always idealized women, intrigued by the magical
qualities they manifest, drawn by their primal power.
Those first clay effigies, always a god*dess*, with full breasts
and plump, ample hips. A highly desirable figure,
representing good fortune, fertile fields, sufficient stores,
no marauders or rival tribes fighting over scant resources.
Women = fecundity, perpetuity, hope in each squalling
babe. Maker of life, giver of pleasure; mentor, muse,
keeper of the ancient wisdom, high priestess of
possibility.

"Land of the Giants" (c. 1971)

Let's pretend a backyard full of stars and those trees over there are really the ruined hull of a crashed spaceship.

Surviving on this strange, new world will be difficult but I appoint myself captain and immediately take command. "We don't know what's out there," I warn my young charges…a necessary precaution, but also to keep them from getting bored.

Creationism (II)

They put me in the Dream Room and turned out all the
lights. Told me to imagineer a universe, with roses and
mosquitoes and platypi. At first I had trouble sleeping, so
they played music and recordings of old stories and
legends. Finally I was drowsy and heard them creep out.
It was dark and completely silent. The stillness at the
onset of sleep. An initial flicker of hypnagogic images: a
ferris wheel, clouds, a dock jutting out into a lake.
Exploded in an instant, erupting from a single point of
light.

A Million Little Pieces

There's no such thing as a "true" story. We—every one of us—fictionalize our lives. Everything is recorded through our senses and, as a result, our perceptions are highly subjective. My recollection of an event will differ sharply from that of other observers. The studies they've done on memory. False memories. Altered memories. Missing memory. *Nothing* we see is factual, everything is processed and interpreted by minds riddled with biases and preconceptions and false conjectures. Memories aren't tactile but they *are* elastic. They're comforting—or terrifying. Or sexy. But each one has been altered in a fundamental way. Edited by time, emotions and physiology. Like film, memory flickers, flutters, grows brittle and, eventually, breaks. Then the burning light.

The Killer Apes

We could be so much more. As a species. Only there's a built-in mechanism: we can only rise so far. A kind of "dead man's switch" left by a Creator worried that its offspring might outstrip them. We fly high but, inevitably, crash *hard*. We are imbued with minds that can posit eleven dimensions. We reverse engineer Creation…to make bombs. Our eyes should be on glory, but our hearts are set on rapine.

Cassini

I'll only allow you my outer atmosphere, resisting when you try to probe deeper. Dissecting me with every spectrum of light. But I devour your robot drones before their telemetry reveals my secrets. A squirt of radiation usually does the trick. To be fair, I must say you're persistent. Five years, ten years, and you're back. A more sophisticated instrument package, directed by a tiny machine brain, wary to a fault. I prepare my defenses and, meanwhile, try to keep up appearances: a gas giant and seemingly devoid of life.

The Word (YHWH)

Deposed like Mithras, a god who *just missed* being as famous as Jesus. Cast out as a demi-urge, one more example of the winners writing history. Once upon a time and in the beginning was the Word. Forbidden and hastily forgotten. Set to trigger the unbinding. Tantalizing while it horrifies, forever on the tip of my tongue.

Toxic Waste

A witch's heart won't burn, so what do you do with it? It can't be buried, its evil influence would still be felt, blighting crops, causing stillbirths. To cast it into a well would poison the water table for miles around.

No, best to keep the vile thing locked away. In a lead-lined canister, sealed with wax, submerged in holy water.

And who better to steward the damned things than me? Serving as an invaluable repository for witch-hunters desperate to dispose of something infernal, indestructible. Making a pretty penny off it too, if I may say so. Not many willing to do the work, to be honest.

It's the shrieking and carrying on that's the worst. There are nights I have to plug up my ears. They never rest and they *never* stop yearning to be free. From a hundred shelves, a thousand faceless jars. Some of them claiming innocence, and they're the most dangerous and insidious of all.

Spirit Photography

Some trace of you still lingers like excreted protoplasm, a memory sticky to the touch.

Things go missing or I find them broken, a whiff of ozone in the air.

I come around the corner and your face materializes before me, contorted by spiritual agony. *Like you are burning...*

And then sometimes you're just a feeling, all but invisible to trusted senses; a shadow on the emulsion, familiar only to discerning eyes.

Viral

You come down with a mild *meme* infection, a dose of something that makes you view life as essentially meaningless. Your existence leaving little or no mark on the rest of the universe. That's what you get for hanging out in chat rooms, swapping spit with virtual strangers. Avatars of famous movie stars, sex kittens or lumbering Lovecraftian monstrosities. Someone left you a malign calling card, a dribble of corrupted code. You feel logy, out of sorts. They're calling it an Apathy Worm and, unfortunately, there doesn't seem to be a cure.

Brutal Fascistic Beatings

Our generation doesn't punish children like our parents did. For one thing, we no longer mete out brutal, fascistic beatings. I mean, hitting repeatedly and hitting to *hurt*. Flailing away at a child, heedless of the force of the blows being inflicted. *Whap, whap, whap.* My father...I don't recall him ever laying a hand on us. One glare with those grey-blue eyes, that's all it took. My mother was the hitter. She had a terrible temper and a miserable life and after a hard day of scraping by, she was an open wound. Advancing on us, wearing a look of absolute fury or possibly even *hate*...

Behind the Mask

Y'know, to be brutally honest about it, I never got along with Superman. None of us did. It was always, like, "well, call if you need me and I'll come bail you out". That kind of thing. And, I gotta say, his grandstanding is pretty hard to swallow. The guy's a born ham! Always hogging the limelight and, of course, that didn't go over well with the rest of us.

I mean…he can move planets, fer Chrissake! Travel faster than the speed of light! And here's us mere mortals running around, taking care of all the two-bit stuff while he waits in the wings, ready to swoop in and save the day, yet again. Supes…hey, give him credit, the guy's indestructible, incorruptible. Totally impervious to *anything*. Although, I gotta tell you, sometimes a few of us would get together and, y'know, raise some tall ones and toss around ideas about taking him down. Y'know, if he turned evil all of a sudden and it was up to us to keep him from running amok. I think it was Bruce Wayne who suggested a "Kryptonite enema". Bruce never could stand him but that's because he's such a prima donna himself. Guy hates to be upstaged. That bat signal of his…total self-promotion.

You gotta wonder if the S-man's ears weren't burning sometimes. 'Cause supposedly he can hear a soap bubble popping in China, right? Maybe that's why he didn't hang around HQ a lot. Basically just dropped in, collected his mail and *phhht*! Back to the Fortress of Solitude. He never came to any of our Christmas parties or stuff like when Spiderwoman got married. That's the way he is. There's only *one* Superman and if the rest of us don't like it, too bad.

And, y'know, that kind of attitude isn't likely to endear you to a guy. I'm not the only one who feels that way either. Hawkman, Green Lantern, you talk to them and they'll tell you the same thing. Believe me, he rubs a lot of people the wrong way. It's just that he's such an icon, the ultimate superhero...no one wants to admit that he's also the world's biggest *shmuck*.

Bully

I hate you. Do you hear me? I said *I hate you*. I hate your guts. You disgust me. Seriously. You need help. A total makeover. I mean, look at you. You're fat and ugly, your face is hideous and your body—well, better not go there. 'Cause there ain't much to work with. You want my advice, get one of those things they make those Arab women wear. It's your only hope. Unless you get lucky and meet some really desperate blind guy.

And it's not just the way you look. There's something *wrong* with you. You creep people out. You should ask yourself, *why does everybody hate me*? Hint: it might have something to do with your total lack of personality. That's...just a guess. Freckles and pimples—and that unibrow. *Gawd*. If you were any uglier, you'd be in a zoo.

I suppose you're gonna start crying now. The old self-pity routine. Like that's going to get you anywhere. Why don't you try cutting yourself again? See if that attracts attention. You're pathetic, you know that? Worse than that, you're *weak*. You're weak and you're all alone, aren't you? No one cares about you, no one wants to be your friend. You might as well be invisible. Wait...where are you? Where did you go? There's no one here. *Gone*. In fact, it's possible you never existed at all...

Loveless

My parents stopped talking about three years ago. I shouldn't exaggerate. They haven't stopped talking *completely*. They don't leave little notes to each other or anything. It's just that it's nothing beyond, y'know, "we need more milk" or "did you pay the power bill". Going through the motions but nothing...never a real conversation. It's *weird*. And you should see their body language if they're in the same room together. For one thing, they stay as far apart as possible and they don't *look* at each other. That's freaky too. And because they don't interact, it's like they have to focus all their attention on *me*, right? And I feel like I'm constantly—like I'm under a microscope. They're looking to me for some kind of...*affirmation* or something. And as long as I keep getting good marks and stay out of trouble, I must be doing all right. Everything's hunky dory. And the scary thing is, I think they really, honestly believe that.

The So-Called "Incident"

First of all, none of this would have happened if Mrs. Steinmetz was still working here. She understood the needs of your average patron. I could go see her and she'd straighten out any problems. Not this Ms. Arnott. She kept saying that, "Miz, Miz, Miz", and I thought she was being totally excessive about it. Miss, Miz, what's the difference? I tried to explain the deal with "Mr. Hulot's Holiday" and I thought I was being really nice about it. I said it was sort of like a ritual with me and explained the arrangement I had with Mrs. Steinmetz which I naturally thought would be continued under the new management. But this Ms. Arnott, she was totally out to lunch on the entire subject. She wouldn't let me reserve "Mr. Hulot". That's what started everything. How mean she was about it. I don't know about you, but I really get my back up when people are rude to me. So I got rude right back. I told her what a disgrace the library had become since Mrs. Steinmetz retired. I said I didn't know if it was because she was Jewish, but Mrs. Steinmetz always seemed to be able to talk to you. I said Mrs. Steinmetz let me reserve "Mr. Hulot's Holiday" over Christmas for the past 7-8 years and that's when Ms. Arnott *really* got snarky and pointed out that it was still only July. *But I was only trying to confirm the previous deal with Mrs. Steinmetz* (who, I'm sure, would be only too happy to verify the truthful veracity of this statement). I'm sorry I got so mad but it was totally her fault. The so-called "incident" was that a stack of books somehow fell over when I was in the vicinity. I might have leaned on them or whatever but I don't think so. *Ms.* Arnott totally lost it at that point and threatened to call the *police* of all people. I don't think it's right that I should be banned from the library over such a trivial thing and that's why I'm approaching you, as board members, to overturn that decision forthwith. Also, I'd like to reserve "Mr. Hulot's Holiday" every Christmas from now on. Which, I think, would eliminate the alleged problem. The video is in pretty bad shape but it's still my favorite movie of all time. Also, I'm sorry things got so out of hand and I promise it won't happen again.

Thank you for your time and thoughtfulness and I sincerely and respectfully await your decision regarding this unfortunate matter. I have told the truth, the whole truth and nothing but the truth and now I would like to put the entire thing behind me. That is all I have to say at this time. Thank you, once again.

Sinned Against

I know what you're thinking. Me being here. Looking like this. Then again, maybe I had it coming to me. Yeah. That would make it easier somehow. If I wasn't a perfect angel. You wonder how I do it. Put up with it night after night. Then, just as suddenly, you decide it's really none of your business. You keep walking and soon put me out of your mind. You can do that. It's a defense mechanism. This automatic reflex that keeps you from feeling bad.

Interview

The manager, a balding guy in his late thirties, looks at me and says, y'know, really casually "you don't have a problem with hard work, do you?". Just like that. And we both know what he's talking about. I mean, it's there, right in front of us. But we won't name it. Him because he's in denial and because he thinks he's doing me a favor just by giving me this interview. A real liberal thinker. And me, I just want a *job*, man. I don't care if it's shoveling coals in hell. If I have to put up with taking crap from the likes of him five days a week, hey, that's fine with me. Just pay me a decent wage, that's all I ask.

I have to wonder what he's basing his attitude on. Has he had bad experiences in the past? Is it one specific group or type of person he doesn't like or is it just anyone who's different? But it really galls me that he assumes someone like me has a different idea of what work is. And the way he's speaking so slowly, like I'm having trouble understanding him.

The main thing is *will he give me a chance*? Already by asking that question he's raised barriers between us. It's not like he's called me any names or done anything wrong. Nothing illegal. He just let down his guard. He isn't sure about me. *My kind*. And it comes to me at that moment: I'm *not* going to get the job. No way. I make him too uncomfortable. It's clear from his obvious reluctance to shake my hand. Almost as if he's afraid my disease can be transmitted by touch.

God's Power for Fathers

My father called them "family compacts". He would summon us to the table, usually after supper, and one by one he'd *list* the many ways we had supposedly wronged him over the past week (or however long it had been). You always hoped that you'd be one of the first. The more he drank, the more abusive he became. By the time he got to the last person, he'd be frothing at the mouth. Years of counseling helped me figure out why he did those things. It was all that underlying frustration and rage. A lifetime of thwarted ambition. We were created in his accursed image and therefore, in his eyes, made from inferior clay.

Hearing Voices

I can hear this little voice in the back of my head going *shut up, Matt, cool it, man* but does that stop me? Nossir. Not for one *minute.* I'm gonna tell this crazy woman what I think of her and that's that. And so I do. I don't hold anything back. I tell her she's fat and not only that, she's stupid and lousy in bed to boot. This great spewing of venom and hate. While she's screaming away in the bathroom, I'm walking out the door, twirling my keys around my finger like the master gunslinger I imagine myself to be. I'm actually getting into my car. Starting it and putting it into gear. Pulling away. From the curb. From my ex-life. Beginning all over again. Easing my old Pontiac into the traffic and going with the flow...

But, y'know, starting a new life is harder than it sounds. I soon find out who my real friends are. Spend more than a few nights sleeping in the car. Can't find a job or a decent place to live. I give serious thought to knocking over a liquor store or 7-11, just to have some *money.* Gradually things come together. I luck into a job with a moving company, which pays the rent (barely) on a bachelor apartment in a building that smells of cat pee and old ladies. Me and Steve-O, we're the A-Team. Bust our butts for ten bucks an hour plus the occasional gratuity for not chipping the paint or manhandling the family china. It's not as bad as it sounds. Except that I'm almost obsessively afraid of hurting my back or dropping something heavy on my foot. Ending up on disability— what sort of compensation is there for a $10 an hour job?

Not even enough to starve on. I'd be out in the street again. No, thanks.

To make a long story short, the months fly by and one day me and Steve-O are sent to this place in the 'burbs. White picket fence, the whole deal. The door opens and there's my *ex*, looking cheerful and perky...until she sees me, at which point her face abruptly changes, becoming more guarded. Steve, of course, has no idea what's going on, blabbering away like he always does. Browning up to her, angling for a bigger tip. He's the master. It's a simple job, really. She wants a freezer moved from the basement out to the garage. Her husband (!) is having their basement converted into a rec room.

Other than some eye contact, she and I never let on we know each other.

Steve-O slips on a tag of carpet as we're going up the stairs and the full weight of the appliance nearly flattens me. I feel a burn in my lower back. Finally he's able to get a handle on it and take some of the load off. "Hey, Matt, you all right?" His head pops up over top of the freezer. "Lost you there for a second."

"Yeah," I groan. "I'm fine." But it's a lie. We wrestle the freezer up the stairs and out to the garage. By the time we push and slide it into place, I'm in trouble. The pull or strain is about belt high and getting worse by the minute. Maybe a few hefty doses of ibuprofen and a heating pad will do the trick. Somehow I doubt it.

Steve-O yaps all the way back. "Nice lady, huh? Foxy too. Her husband's a lucky guy. Hey, how's your back, partner?" Sitting has only made it worse. I'm stiffening up. I doubt I'll be able to get out of the truck without help.

I know karma at work when I see it. Cosmic forces have conspired to bring this about. I'm paying for the sins I committed against her. For the cruelty I knowingly inflicted. I feel bad enough...but, wouldn't you know it, there's that annoying little voice again, only this time all it says is: *told you so*.

Mid-Life Crisis

How old do you have to be before you realize...wait, that's not...I'll try it again, okay?

(Pause)

At some point, it dawns on you. No, it's more like one day you have this epiphany that shakes you right to your soul. What it is is that you come to understand that things aren't going to improve, there aren't going to be any miraculous...it's not like you're going to win a lottery and, y'know, everything's all of a sudden perfect, okay? It doesn't work like that. There's nothing waiting in the wings to save you, no *deus ex machina* is gonna reach down, hoist you up and carry you off to a better place.

It reminds me of that Talking Heads song: you look around and you say to yourself *this isn't my house, this isn't my life.* Somewhere, maybe in a parallel universe, someone is living the life you were meant to have. And in that universe tomorrow will be different and better than today. And...that's just not the way it is for you. You're alone now and you'll be alone tomorrow. You hate your job and you always will. You want to change but you never will. You *ache* for someone or something to redeem you, but at the same time can't quite shake the conviction that you probably don't deserve it.

Death Wish

It's getting to the point where you're actively *looking* for things: bumps, cysts, any kind of enlargement or strange swelling. You're occasionally bothered by phantom pains, in your stomach and lower back. At night you get these sharp twinges in your chest. And lately that irritable bowel of yours has gotten downright cranky, hasn't it? When are you going to see someone about *that*, submitting meekly to the indignities *that* entails? And what will you say about the other stuff and will you tell your doctor your suspicions regarding your pancreas?

How do you explain what you're feeling? It's hard to put into words so you avoid mentioning it on those rare occasions when you require the services of the avuncular Dr. Tillman. You don't want to sound like a hypochondriac. Meanwhile you're *Googling* your symptoms and poring over the family's medical encyclopedia, reading about all sorts of cancers and wasting illnesses, marveling at their sheer nastiness. You imagine being told, actually hearing the words as you believe they would be spoken by Tillman. How would you react? Who would you tell first? What would you do with the weeks or months you had left?

Crazy-making questions but by this time you've gone too far to turn back, it's become an obsession to follow it through to the end. So tomorrow or the next day you find yourself calling funeral homes, telling some made-up story, checking on arrangements and prices but, really, more interested in the gory details.

Anchorite

The first one is a kook. Total whack job.

Rings the doorbell and right away starts babbling about ley lines and planetary convergences, everything explained by this crude chart he holds up for perusal. And all the while keeping his eyes cast down because he's afraid of being "blinded by immanence" or something like that. It's hard to make out what he's saying because he's weeping, practically vibrating from a combination of fear and excitement. The guy won't be talked down or dissuaded. Eventually he wanders off, pausing every once in awhile to shout and point at the house. Weird.

But the word must be out because another one shows up the next day, an old man who won't approach the door. Content to stand at the end of the walk, bracing himself on a cane when the arthritis in his hip gets too bad. He's there until dark. And then he's gone.

More arrive daily, most content to be bystanders, others bolder. There are all kinds of places on the internet. Conspiracy theorists and cultists and people who believe the apocalypse is due a week from Thursday.

A particularly awkward moment when a woman thrusts out an infant, screaming: "Heal him! Don't let him die!" Closing the door but she won't stop screaming. Rushing out to calm her, reason with her. And the whole time it's "my baby, my baby", the neighbors looking on with frank disapproval.

It gets worse. A steady stream of people arriving, knocking at all hours. The congestion creating a parking and traffic nightmare. It's a quiet neighborhood and residents start to complain.

The police and authorities are, predictably, completely unhelpful. Initially dubious, suspecting some kind of publicity stunt. They check around, find the sites in question. Someone alerts the media, which means *more* unwanted attention, phone calls, requests for interviews. The situation only exacerbated when the Pope becomes involved, issuing a statement denouncing superstition and idolatry.

Uniformed officers are stationed around the clock, an attempt to keep the growing throng under control. Weapons have been seized, along with extremist literature and bizarre religious tracts. The situation quickly deteriorating.

Late one night, someone breaks through the cordon. Presses his face to the door, whimpering: "*Libera me, Domine*" and, as he is dragged away, howling: "*Miserere mei, Deus!*"

Living like a prisoner now, unable to venture outside or peer from a window. And day and night, 24/7, serenaded by a continual soundtrack of prayers and hymns. Someone even sets up a loudspeaker and plays amplified recordings of rabbits being slaughtered and children crying—o, pity the suffering children.

Unplug the telephone, turn off the lights, sit in the dark. They'll weary of this eventually, go back to their homes. Give them nothing to encourage their simple credulity. Alone and besieged. Resigned and dangerously bored. Reorganizing the cupboards and bookshelves, performing a thousand small chores. Playing endless games of solitaire and, naturally, winning every single time.

Accident

This is a car crash. It's happening *right now*. A collision in progress. Metal folding and bending, glass slow-motion bursting, bodies swaying in their seats. And the thing is you see it with *perfect* clarity, high-def to the max. You watch with fascination as the airbag blooms in front of you, a time-lapse explosion expanding toward your face as you lean forward to meet it. Something else. A heaviness. In the region of your chest. A tug in your neck that isn't *quite* pain but soon will be. A sound, a soft exhalation but really a scream in the midst of being born. From the backseat. Ten A.U.'s behind you. Any moment now it will all come rushing in, a cacophony of distress, a *wall* of noise and sensations. Someone, maybe even you, might be in the process of dying. On the threshold of an instant. The invisible lip of an event horizon. Falling ...and forever suspended mere petaseconds away from nothing at all.

First Words

"My health was endangered. Terror assailed me."
Arthur Rimbaud, on the writing of *Illuminations*

Franz Kafka insisted we should only read books that "bite and sting us". Volumes, one presumes, capable of savaging unwary readers, leaving them spotted with blood. Kafka, a gentle man, left strict instructions in his will that his writings be *burned*. His executor, Max Brod, ignored his friend's wishes and preserved his distinctive novels and stories; as a result, I frequently risk serious injury plucking them from my shelves.

Words created us and words sustain us:

> "The technical language of religion is
> symbolism, with storytelling one of its
> most important varieties."
> (so sayeth Huston Smith)

Ideas become words become action. The correct conjunction of vowels and consonants will, according to some mythologies, lead to an *unbinding*.

A return to nullity. From whence we came.

Be mindful and compassionate. Practice right thought, right speech. Do not call the worst into being. Offer prayers to a Creator beyond faith. Use the ancient words of praise. The ones handed down through the ages. *Hallowed be thy name, o, Lord, thy will be done...*

Occupy

We rally beneath a makeshift banner, take to the streets in droves. A revolution without leaders, the spontaneous groundswell sweeping away the old guard, old modes. The tyranny of capitalism and the mindless braying of its desperate hawkers.

An ideology based on LIFE, eschewing hedonism for sustainability. Laws, codes, rulebooks struck down, superseded by the One Over-Arching Principle: "Good food, Clean Water, Fresh Air".

Selling off the Vatican, bulldozing the Pentagon, auctioning the Taj Majal. Redistributing ill-gotten gains. In despair, former oil executives turn themselves into human hand grenades. But we are not deterred. The actions of a few misguided terrorists will not dissuade us from our task, our mission.

We exile the Incorrigibles, placing our trust in generations still to come. We belong to the future and kill yesterday in the wink of an eye.

Faggot

"Bagshaw," my father says suddenly. He's been silent nearly an hour and his voice gives me a start.

"What was that, Dad?"

"Who I was talking about." Shooting me a stern look. "The little queer." I don't remember any reference to *Bagshaw* but, never mind; clearly he's been off on some kind of mental ramble. "Worked at head office with me. A swish, and not ashamed to flaunt it either." He pauses to get his breath. His lips are dry and grey. Everything in the process of shutting down. Propped up to help him breathe, Demerol to handle the pain. He's making a sound, wheezing, could it be...*laughter?* "Lord, how I tormented that man."

"What did you do?"

His face is still drawn but animated by something that looks suspiciously like a smirk. "I'd put thumbtacks and pins on his chair. Not every day, spacing it out so he'd always be caught off guard. I was down the hall but I could hear him squeal. Served him right." I'm leaning forward, fists *clenched*. Make myself ease back in the chair, force open my furious hands. He angles his head toward me. His eyes sunken, lusterless. Dark holes in his face. "Other things too. I'd send him flowers, have them delivered right to his office. With a card. *Love, Charlie* or whatever."

"You're kidding." I can't help it, blurting it out.

"Sure." His thin smile confirming it.

I haven't seen this side of him before; I've often found him thoughtless but never believed him capable of out-and-out malice. "You hated him that much?"

"He made me *sick*. And I wasn't the only one. But I was the sneakiest." A sly wink. "I'd call him, late at night."

"Call him…"

"Never from home. Sometimes from other cities. He'd change his number, get an unlisted one…" His face crinkling with mirth. "Didn't matter. I *worked* with the guy. In Human Resources, no less. *Jesus.* I knew where the bodies were buried and how to find them. That's why I lasted so long." He gestures for the water glass and I automatically move to comply. Holding it for him while he sips through a straw. One final indignity he must endure.

"What would you say," I ask, once he's done, "when you called him?"

"Sometimes nothing. Just letting him know I was still out there. Other times I'd be all…uh…y'know…*you queer, you dirty, little faggot…you'll get what's coming to you.* Just spooking him." I back away, fumbling behind me for the chair. Then I realize I still have the glass and must rise once more, replacing it on the nightstand beside the bed. Finding it difficult to approach him again, this stranger I've known all my life.

"What was his first name?"

"What? I don't recall. He only lasted a year."

"He quit?"

"Couldn't take it, I guess." There's no remorse, that's the thing. He's talking about running over a dog in the street, thirty years after the fact.

"And then you left him alone? Or—"

"Hell, no." Frowning at his foolish son. "That might look suspicious, give him ideas. I kept at it for six more months. Just to be on the safe side…" He's fading again, ebbing away. "Old *Fag*shaw..." Yawning. "You know, the bastard actually *lisped?*"

My father is sixty-four years old and staunchly conservative. A self-made man. In our house, he was the one who held the reins and cracked the whip. Stern but fair, I guess you could say. My sister sees it differently; she believes mom worked and worried herself to death trying to please him.

I should tell him. Right now. Go over and *spit* it right into his face. Just to see his reaction. *God.* Wouldn't that be something? I'm dying to tell him, I'm *about* to tell him...but at that moment his mouth sort of sags open and my dying father begins to snore.

The Many Names of God

I like Philip K. Dick's term: *Vast Active Living Intelligence System* (VALIS). At least it gives some idea of the kind of scale we're talking about. Divine powers of creation that can birth galactic super-clusters and knit it all together with a physics so neat and concise it can very nearly be reduced to an equation. A few numbers and letters that denote paradigm shifts.

Some religions and belief systems hedge around the naming or depiction of their gods and/or lords of creation. Superstition...or an acute understanding of the power of words? The periodic table, after all, nothing more than rows of nonsensical letters that, when properly arranged, become *us*.

Acknowledgements:

A number of these pieces were previously published in the volumes *That First, Wound-Bearing Layer* (Greensleeve Editions; 1992), *Genuinely Inspired Primitive* (Earth Prime Productions; 1993), *violins in the void* (Black Dog Press; 1996) and in various magazines and publications around the world. Others have appeared on my blog, *Beautiful Desolation*.

The "prose poem" format was a godsend to me. Back in the early 1990's, enduring a *horrific* writing drought on Baffin Island (no, I'm not kidding), I started reading work by Charles Baudelaire, Arthur Rimbaud and some of the surrealists. Self-contained snippets that spoke of terrible, profound, disturbing things, dissected and parsed the universe, disclosed hidden realities…and managed to do all that in less than a thousand words.

Many of the works in this volume are the product of "automatic writing", no pre-planning, just putting pen to paper and letting pure inspiration determine what happens next. I am frequently astonished where these stories take me and what they reveal about my fears and preoccupations. At times, they are Rorschach tests, manifestations of my slavering, uncontrollable id. Such efforts can be unsettling (even for the author).

Special thanks and appreciation to my wife, Sherron, who continues to fill the thankless roles of first reader and editor, the very model of patience and tolerance. These short tales cover a lot of ground and range over many years and Sherron has been right there beside me, every step of the way. A companion, partner and friend; a soul mate and so much more.

And thanks, as well, to the readers who've sought me out and subjected themselves to my odd oeuvre. I haven't made it easy for you, have I? And I promise you, I never will.

C.B.
(June, 2012)

Cliff Burns is the author of numerous books, including *The Last Hunt*, *So Dark the Night*, *Of the Night* and *Righteous Blood*. He has been a professional writer since 1985 and lives in western Canada with his wife and two sons.